For my Gwen

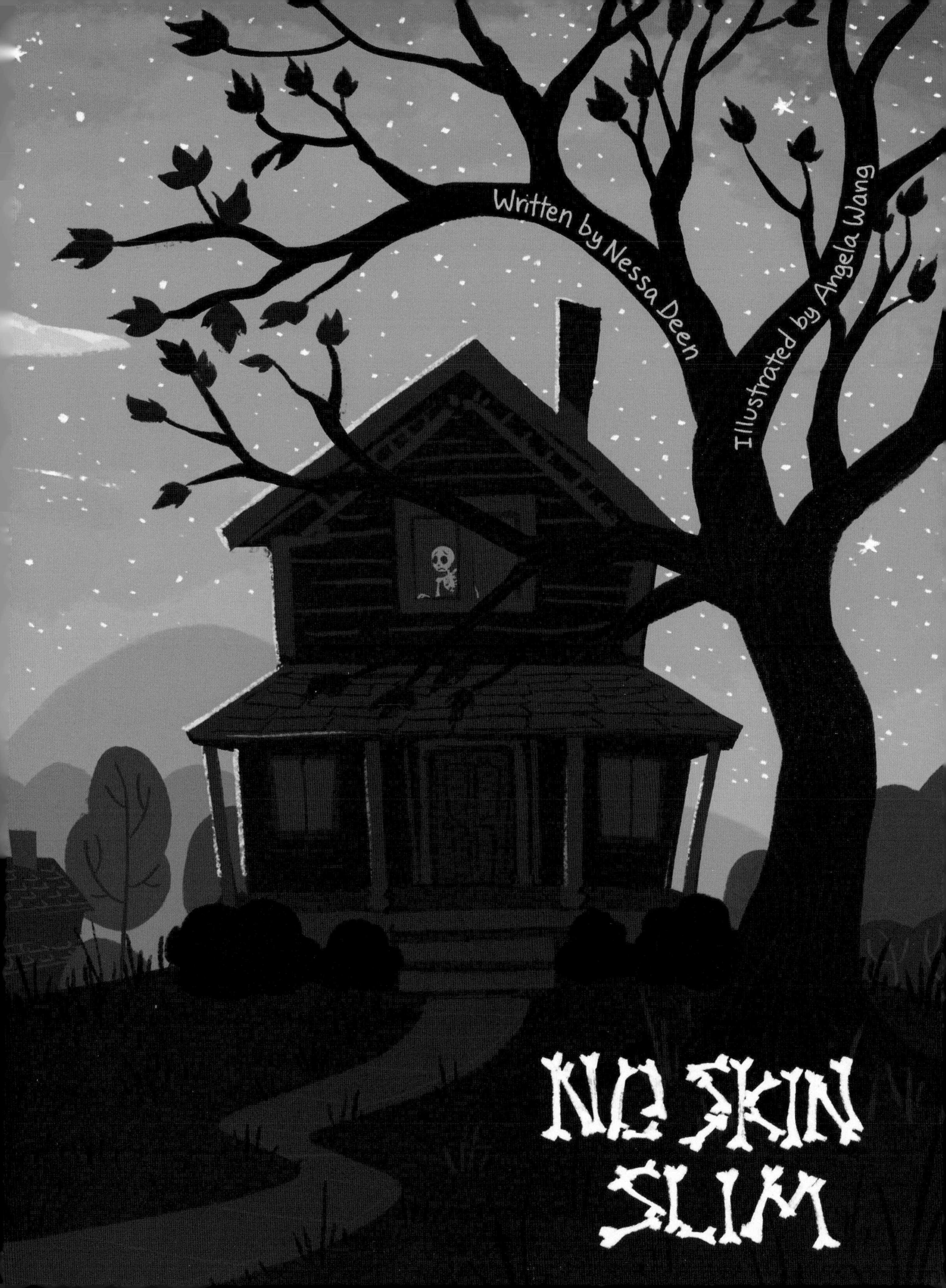

Written by Nessa Deen

Illustrated by Angela Wang

NO SKIN SLIM

It was already dark when Slim first heard footsteps.

Robbers were rummaging around!

The bedroom door creaked open and two of them crept in!

He crouched down low in his closet and hoped that they...

would... go... away.

Slim was scared.

His whole body clicked and clattered.

"This will be your room,"
a big robber said.

A little one, in a mask,
slipped into Slim's bed!

Slim
peered at them through
a crack in the door
and clicked
and clattered
even more.

"What's that noise?" whispered the little robber.

"It's an old house," the big one said very quietly.
"Old houses make sounds. It's time to go to sleep.
Tomorrow, the moving van will be here
and you will have your bike again."

The
light
flicked
off.

Slim
waited.

An
hour
went
by,

then
two,

then
three.

Slim pushed the closet door open,
hunched his bumpy back, and made a break for it!

The light flicked... on!

Slim froze on his toes in a rickety pose.

"Aaaaahhhh!!! A robber!!!!!!"

"Aaaaahhhh!!! A monster!!!!!!!"

"I'm not a robber. I'm a kid," said the kid.

"Well, I'm not a monster," snapped Slim.
"I'm a skeleton."

The kid was skeptical. "Why is a skeleton hiding in the closet like a monster?"

Slim scowled. "Because you scared me!"

"Why are you...
sneaking around my room...
in a mask...
like a robber?"

"These?... These are my
'Gus the Great' pajamas," the kid said.

"We just moved here.

My name is Gus."

No one had been in the house but Slim for many, many years.

It would be nice to finally have a friend, he thought.

"My bike is coming tomorrow," said Gus.

"If you share your room, I will share my bike."

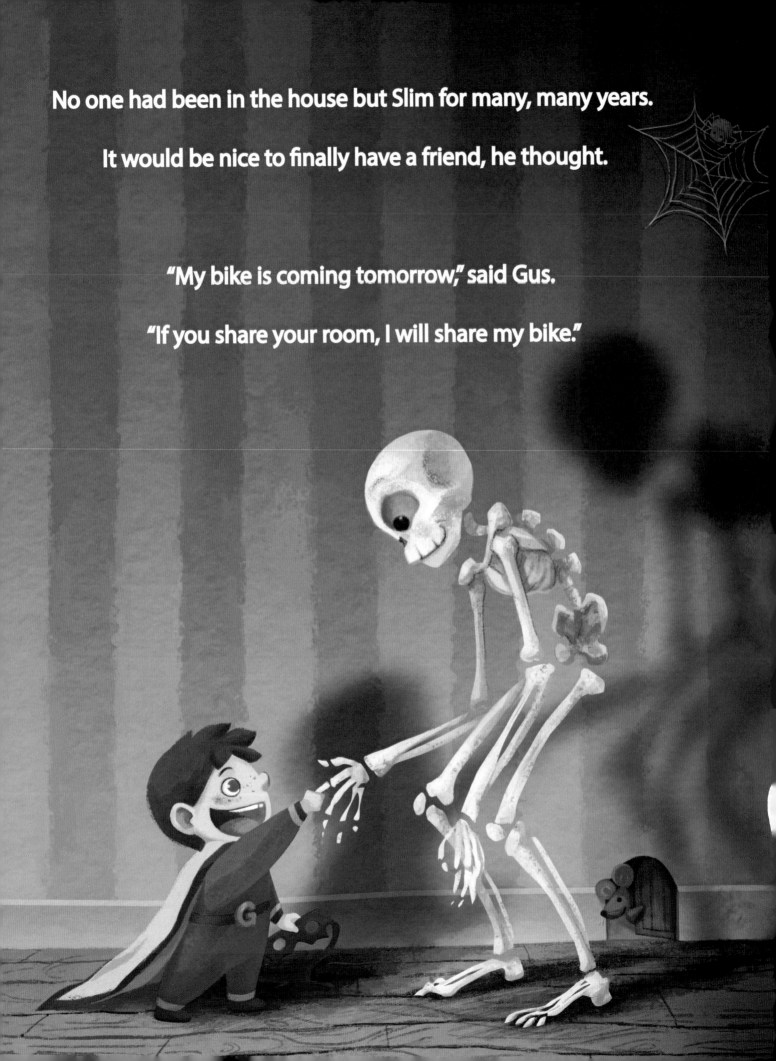

Slim could not believe it!
All his life he wanted
to ride a bike!

"It's a deal!" he exclaimed.

"My name is Slim
and I like bikes!"

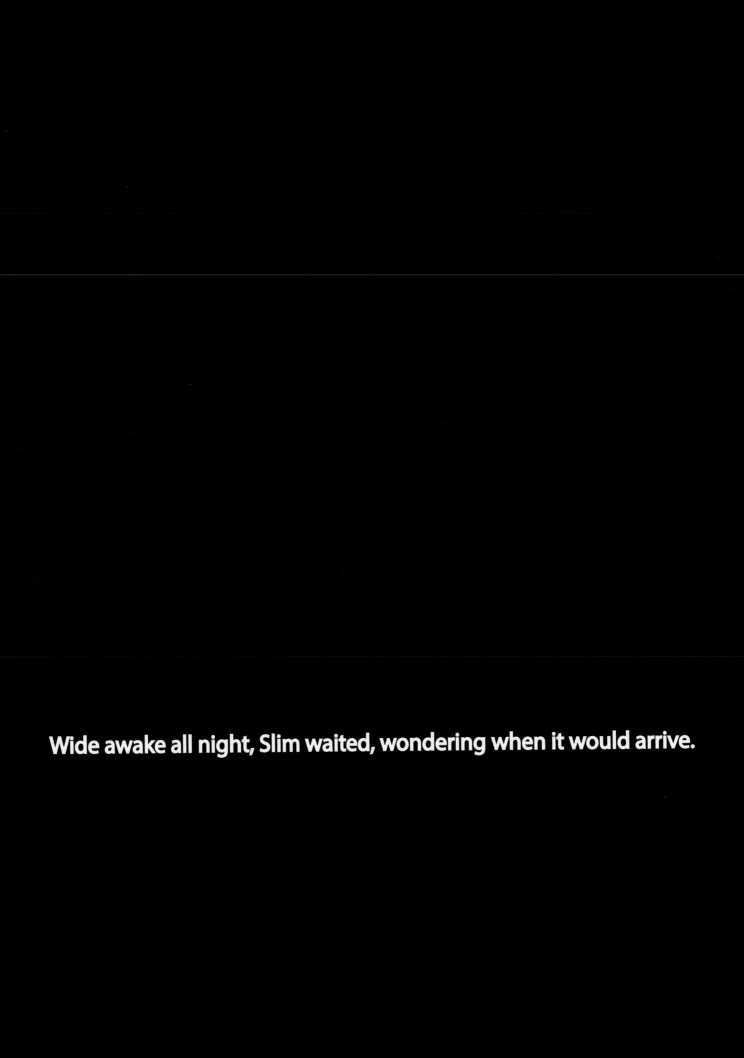

Wide awake all night, Slim waited, wondering when it would arrive.

Honk! Honk!

A moving van
pulled up and parked.

Seven men began bringing
in boxes and a bright, blue bike
with special, sparkly spokes.

"It's here!" shouted Slim.

"Shhhh," Gus shushed.
"You shouldn't shout.
Someone might see you.

And you... are a little creepy looking."

Slim studied himself in the mirror.
"Huh? Creepy looking? Me?"

"Yes," said Gus.
"You don't have any skin."

Slim had never thought about that before.
He didn't feel creepy.
"Is skin important?" he asked.

"It sure is!" assured Gus.

"What if I smile?" Slim suggested.
"Everybody likes a smile."
He opened his mouth very wide
and showed off all his teeth.

Gus gasped. "Do not do that! It does not help!
You have no lips. It only makes you creepier.
You need skin."

Slim's shoulders slouched.

"Don't worry, Slim. Gus the Great will get you some skin."

Gus came back
a little while later with...

Tin Foil!

Gus tucked Slim up with tin foil and then stepped back.

"You look super, Slim! Like a knight in shining armor
and knights aren't creepy, they are brave."

"Yeah!" cheered Slim. "Let's go!"

As they marched down the stairs,
a moving man nodded at them.

Slim waved hello,
as a good warrior would,
but worried they'd notice
he had no lips... as he should.

Outside they went. Slim was so excited.
He could see the sunshine glinting all around him.

Just then, a bird flew down
and plucked a strip of tin foil.

Then another flew down.

And.. another!

And... another!

"Oh, no!" shouted Gus.
"Your bones are showing!"

He threw a cardboard box over Slim.

"Let's go home. We can try again."

Slim sat sadly in the bedroom.

"Don't worry, Slim. Gus the Great will get you some skin."

Gus came back a little while later with...

Shaving cream!

Gus squirted Slim with shaving cream and then stepped back.

"You look super, Slim! Like a clumpy cloud and clouds aren't creepy, they are floofy!"

"Yeah!" cheered Slim. "Let's go!"

Plopping blobs of sloppy glop, they headed down the hall.

Outside they went. Slim was so excited.

Grassy tufts and dandelion puffs poked up between his toes.

Suddenly, the sprinklers went off, spraying water
across the yard and washing away the shaving cream.

"Oh no!" shouted Gus. "Your bones are showing!"

He threw a cardboard box over Slim.
"Let's go home. We can try again."

Slim sank sullenly in the bedroom.

"Don't worry, Slim. Gus the Great will get you some skin."

Gus came back a little while later with...

Yarn!

Gus wrapped and wound and wove Slim up
in the woolly yarn and then stepped back.

"You look super, Slim! Like a puffy pillow,
and pillows aren't creepy, they are poofy."

"Yeah!" cheered Slim.
"Let's go!"

"I like your sweater," said Gus's Mommy as they cut through the kitchen. "Do you live around here?"

Slim nodded. "Yes, very close."

"Would you like to stay for lunch?" she offered. "I'm making spaghetti and meatballs. It's Gus's favorite."

"No, thank you. I don't eat," Slim said, politely.

Outside they went. Slim was so excited.

He diggity-digged a little jig along the sidewalk and didn't notice the yarn snag on a broken branch.

As he danced away, the yarn unspun behind him.

"Oh, no!" shouted Gus.

"Your bones are showing!"

He threw a cardboard box over Slim.

Spaghetti and meatballs!

"We had a lot of leftovers after lunch."

Gus squished and squashed the spaghetti all over Slim and then stepped back.

"You look super, Slim! Like a giant plate of spaghetti and meatballs... and spaghetti isn't creepy, it's my favorite!"

"Yeah!" cheered Slim. "Let's go!"

Gus felt positive this was an A+ plan. Nothing is more amazing than a noodle man!

Slim indeed agreed.

Outside they went. Slim was so excited.
He could feel the wind whoosing by
as he wobbled down the sidewalk.

Out of nowhere, a skinny dog
with a pointy nose,
scurried over and licked Slim's toes.

Then, a shabby, shaggy dog
shuffled in and licked Slim's shin.

And a bouncy, barking dog
bounded by and licked
Slim's thigh!

"Oh, no!" shouted Gus. "Your bones are showing!"
He threw a cardboard box over Slim. "Let's go home."

Slim

sobbed

softly

in the bedroom.

Gus the Great had done it again!

He knew the solution to help his new friend!

It sat on his nose the night they moved in!

"Yeah!" cheered Slim. "Let's go!"

Outside they went.

Slim was so excited!

So, so excited.

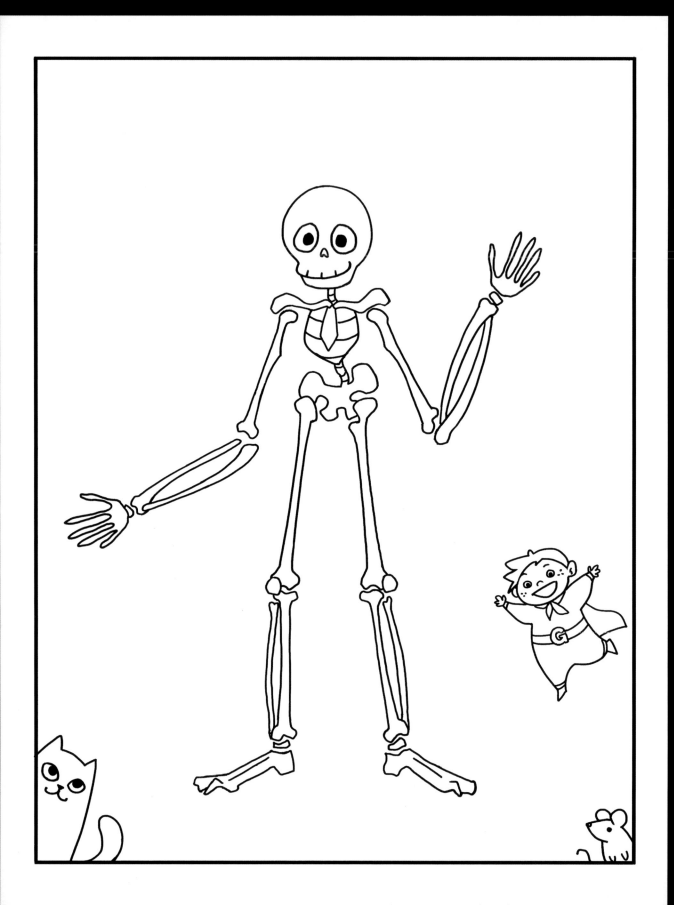

How would you cover Slim?